WHEN YOU'RE A
ZOMBIE

My name is Zander and I'm a zombie. People think they know what it's like to be a zombie, but they don't!

When you are a zombie, people think you are gray but that's not true! You can be purple, blue, or even pink!

I have green skin.

When you are a zombie, people think you eat brains, but we don't! We eat a variety of foods.

Breadsticks and pizza are my favorite!

HALLOWEE

When you are a zombie, people think you are slow, but that's not true! Some of us are very fast!

I run on the track team at school!

When you are a zombie, people think you can only come out at night, but that's not true! I love being outside during the day!

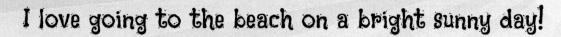

I love going to the beach on a bright sunny day!

When you are a zombie, people think you live in a graveyard, but we don't!

I live in a nice little house in town.

When you are a zombie, people think you will be mean and scary, but all aren't.

There can be nice zombies and mean zombies, just like people! I'm not mean. I just want to say hello.

When you are a zombie, people think you don't trick-or-treat, but we do.

Halloween is my favorite time of year!

When you are a zombie, people think we walk with our arms stuck out to catch people, but that's not true!

We walk with our arms out because it helps us balance. Zombie brains are just different than other people's brains and that's ok!

When you are a zombie, people think you don't recognize your family, but that's not true! We have strong family bonds.

Every Saturday my family gets together to play Zombie football.

When you are a zombie, people think we don't care about our clothes, but that's not true!

I hate being dirty. I always change into clean clothes after soccer practice.

When you are a zombie, people think our bones stick out. Well, that can be true for some of us, like my mom!

When you are a zombie, people think our limbs fall off, but they don't.

All of our limbs stay intact.

When you are a zombie, people think you have cold skin, and don't feel the cold, but that's not true!

I get hot and cold just like you do.

When you are a zombie, people think we are solitary creatures, but that's not true.

HALLOWEEN

We are just misunderstood and want to be friends.

Made in United States
North Haven, CT
28 August 2023

40862604R00020